MUFFLE

AARCHI ADVANI SAINI

Copyright © Aarchi Advani Saini
All Rights Reserved.

This book has been published with all efforts taken to make the material error-free after the consent of the author. However, the author and the publisher do not assume and hereby disclaim any liability to any party for any loss, damage, or disruption caused by errors or omissions, whether such errors or omissions result from negligence, accident, or any other cause.

While every effort has been made to avoid any mistake or omission, this publication is being sold on the condition and understanding that neither the author nor the publishers or printers would be liable in any manner to any person by reason of any mistake or omission in this publication or for any action taken or omitted to be taken or advice rendered or accepted on the basis of this work. For any defect in printing or binding the publishers will be liable only to replace the defective copy by another copy of this work then available.

Contents

Foreword

Before spearheading into reading the story, resonate the following question in your mind. What quality of the Homo Sapiens laid the foundation for survival of humanity for such a long period? What keeps the people running? Some might say its love that drives us to thrive. Some say its courage that enables explore new things and pushes us forward. There are many poetic answers available for the question asked. Let us put those theories to test with this story.

Aarchi Advani Saini.!

    [ ] Author of the book "The Loads Of Poetry"
    [ ] Social media "Aarchi Advani Saini"
    [ ] Aries, believe in destiny.

[ ] Author of the book "The Loads Of Poetry Part One and Two", "The Journey of Love", "The Way to Love", "The Anonymous", "Let's be Confidante", "New Self", "Error", "The Cabalistic Child ", "Confession", "Dark Dead", "Half Dead", "Faith is All", "Anjaan Ajnabi", "Lifeless Life", " Dream", and more.

Aarchi was born in India in 25th March 2002, the daughter of Sanjeev Advani Saini and his wife Mamta Saini.

She becomes one of the youngest author of her hometown Shamli. For this Danik Jagran newspaper covers this news, Later, many news channels interviewed her. So renowned for "The loads of poetry). She has sold the book worldwide, the recipient of numerous prestigious awards in her writing journey. She writes daily columns syndicated throughout the world. Aarchi Advani is well known for her writing on many other platforms. She is also a fantasy and literary fiction author specializing in "Life", as well as her upcoming book "Believe".

She publish her 10th book as her Hindi novel called "papa".

She also hosts a channel where she uses her passion for storytelling. And a background in business to help other creatives navigate their writing. So she is compiling an anthology named, "Of Your Choice", And her publishing journey is another level, she is good at her writing skills, but no one knows how to write books, same with her, but with the passage of time, she grows. When she's not writing or tubing she enjoys listening to books,

Making stories on her own. And love to live in her virtual world.

1

Before spearheading into reading the story, resonate the following question in your mind. What quality of the Homo Sapiens laid the foundation for survival of humanity for such a long period? What keeps the people running? Some might say its love that drives us to thrive. Some say its courage that enables explore new things and pushes us forward. There are many poetic answers available for the question asked. Let us put those theories to test with this story.

Long, long ago. Almost 40,000 years ago.

In the vast expanded plains of Europe.

A horde of humans, not the modern age humans exactly, was on move on the vast expanded plain lands of Europe. They were called Cro-Magnons. They carried out that expedition in search of a place for them to survive. Wherever they went the drought chased them back like scavenging vulture, waiting to devour them. The climate change happened during that time had drastic effect on their tribe. The plain lands became waste lands, hardly any vegetation grew there. Due to lack of food and the problem of predators they were driven away from the plane lands.

The Cro-Magnons were tall, mildly built and stood straight. They wore clothing made of animal skins and they carried tools with them. They carried spears made of stones and bones. The group moved in the shape of parcel's head, in the front was the captain of the tribe. He looked strong, tall, had long hair and carried a saw made of crocodile jaw. The tribesmen called him by name 'El'. He led the tribe in the search for safer place where food and water were available for all of them. On the sides of the formation, there were seekers. The seekers were responsible to keep an eye for plausible attack from predators. The seekers carried spear in their hand and always kept them schlepped towards periphery to parry the beasts.

Inside the formation were the other men and women of the tribe, who were comparatively weak and easily susceptible to ambush. Amidst them walked our protagonist. Unlike other Cro-Magnons, he was not so tall and sturdy. He was lean and frail, barely had enough strength to walk. He wore hide of yak as cloth, had long hair and carried no weapon. He was called 'Muffle' by others in his tribe. Yes, you guessed right, he cannot talk and produce any sound. He was born that way. Though he had his short comings, he had this raging desire in his heart to prove himself useful for the tribe. Unfortunately, he had no strength to fend off predators and hunt woolly mammoth for food. He was waiting for his opportunity to prove his worth. Like how the water flows in the path etched on ground, the tribe blindly followed the trail led by their captain.

The sun called it a day and began descending into night. The wind and gale blow hard, uprooting trees. The thunder rumbled and lightning ruled the night sky. There was no cave or cavern found within eyesight. El gathered his tribe together and instructed them to drowse. Some of the tribe's men took the duty of night watch and guarded the tribe while they rested their wearied eyes.

At once the sun went down, the whole place became silent. The blanket of darkness covered the land, blindfolding the Cro-Magnons. The raving wind rendered their attempt of making fire futile. Dropping the idea of making fire the tribe went to sleep. They were used to sleep in the rough terrain and in rough climatic conditions. The howling wind sung a folklore in the ears of Cro-Magnons. In a while, the place fell dead silent and the gale halted without trace. The people of the tribe were sound asleep except one. Muffle was still awake. The air was cold and filled his lungs with ice. After walking through dead land for days without food and water, he was exhausted and tired. But his mind kept him restless. 'What if we cannot find a congenial place to live. What if we were doomed to die in this wasteland?' thoughts filled Muffle's mind. All those thoughts disturbed him. He did not know exactly what the feeling was, but he hated it. Laying down in the ground, gazing at the bright stars he mused, 'Will the gods come do

wn from the sky to save us?'. He got no answers for his questions. He closed his eyelids and tried to get some sleep.

Sleep slowly creeped over him. In his dream, he led his tribe to a place which almost matched heaven. The land was filled with water and vegetation. One can say he was happy as he was smiling in sleep. Sadly, his dream did not last long. He heard clamouring noise and woke up suddenly. He stood up and opened his eyes wide open to look into the event. His vision was blurred as he was just awake. It took him few seconds to acquire perfect vision. When he regained his sight, he saw a sabre tooth tiger circling him. It was covered with thick fur, had curved fangs of steel protruding out of mouth. It's eyes glowed white in the moon light. Sabre tooth tigers hunt in pack. They hunt the weakest in a group and this beast had fixed its eyes on Muffle. Muffle had nothing to defend and looked around for help. The night watchers were fighting other sabre tooths.

"Muffle!" yelled one of the men of his tribe. That man threw a spear to Muffle. Muffle caught the spear with his two hands. "Kill it." yelled the man again. Muffle turned towards the tiger. He looked the tiger in eye, preparing himself to kill it. The tiger glared back, slowly moving towards him. At once the sabre tooth pounced towards him. Muffle thought of plunging the spear through the beast's heart mid-air. When he looked at the magnificent creature coming at him, he had that feeling again. It was fear. His mind instructed him to drive the spear into the tiger, but his heart did not accept the appeal of mind. His hands trembled and he pulled himself back to parry the attack. Alas! He was too slow. The beast tackled him down and stomped one of its feet over his chest. It growled at the prey lying down defenceless. Muffle laid under the feet of the beast, too afraid to do anything.

When the tiger went to grab his neck, El hacked the tiger with his saw. The head of the tiger parted from its body and fell down on the ground. El roared loudly. His roar reverberated through the deserted land. The pack of tigers scattered and ran away into the night swept darkness.

El pulled Muffle up on his feet. "Why did you hold back?" El enquired Muffle. Muffle signed him that he held back because he was afraid. El grinned and started speaking, "Fear? That's good. Control the fear and make it a weapon, otherwise you cannot survive."

When the crisis was averted, the whole tribe went back to sleep. Those advice given by El hit Muffle hard. "How can I control fear and make it a weapon?" mused Muffle.

The next day.

The tribe was back at its routine of searching for their dream world. The dream of the tribesmen was not to have a lavish life or to live like a god. Their dream was to have a place where they can survive. It was so simple as it is.

Muffle was travelling from the middle, still thinking about the thing he learned yesterday. His mind was preoccupied with his thoughts and his legs strode involuntarily along with his tribe. Right away the tribe stopped moving. Muffle heard uproar from the front. The sound was filled with happiness. Yes! They found what they needed. At distance, El saw a vegetation, which was sign of food and water.

The tribe dropped their formation and ran towards the forest screaming in joy. The forest was filled with tall trees rising high, touching the sky. Streams of water leading to river. The trees bestowed them with delicious fruits and chilling shadow. Muffle ran towards the river, he knelt down on ground by the river bank. After months of not witnessing water and food, that sight looked like art to him. Every Cro-Magnons rushed to trees and river, eating all they could and slurping in water.

With face lit up with joy, muffle looked at the surface of the water. He saw the reflection of his face on the surface of water and laughed at it. Suddenly his eye noticed something strange. He also saw the reflection of something up in trees. It jumped from the trees towards him. He swiftly swerved to his side averting the direct attack. That creature landed on the place where he knelt down, if he hadn't moved the impact would have killed him. But many others were not so lucky as him. Many such creatures jumped down from trees upon the Cro-Magnons. They precisely landed on the back of the Cro-Magnons, killing them with the impact. El and many of his tribe warded off the attack like Muffle. El schlepped his saw towards them and looked at the creatures that took out many Cro-Magnons. During his time leading the tribe, El fought many ferocious creatures that possessed threat like sabre tooths, mammoths and many. But he never expected a face off like this. The attack was made by Neanderthals. They were sister species of Cro-Magnons, almost similar like Cro-Magnons but primitive. They had big stub head with broad torso and flat feet. They walked on two feet like Cro-Magnons but Neanderthals were comparatively shorter. The Neanderthals screamed at the Cro-Magnons, intimidating them. El ordered his tribe to fight back. The Cro-Magnons roared at the Neanderthals and the brawl started. Their fight shook the forest and rendered the birds and animals restless and frightened.

The Cro-Magnons tried to kill the Neanderthals with their spears, saws and other tools. But Neanderthals moved swiftly climbing over trees and attacked them from height. While running away from the Neanderthals, Muffle stumbled over a boulder and feel down. Beside him was a Cro-Magnon fighting the Neanderthals. A Neanderthal pounded on him from a tree and tackled him down on the ground. The neanderthal took a boulder and crushed the head of the Cro-Magnon with it. The blood splattered all over the Neanderthal and Muffle who was nearby. The Neandertal's attention turned towards Muffle and screamed at him. Muffle was afraid. He wanted to turn the fear to weapon but he did not know how. He toted his arm against the Neanderthal. The neanderthal screamed at him again, but there was no sound from Muffle. The Neanderthal left Muffle unharmed and climbed up a nearby tree. "Fall back! Get to the plain grounds." Yelled El. The Cro-Magnons retreated and Muffle ran along with them.

The Cro-Magnons were wounded and many were killed. Muffle sat down on the ground processing the event in his mind. "I could have saved him, but let him die. How can I turn the fear into weapon?" thoughts pondered his mind. He spent hours thinking about the question that keeps him up at night. Slowly the answer started flowing to his mind. The fear is a thing that helps life survive. The fear makes the life crave for power and power won't come easily. The proof of power is struggle and to overcome struggle we need a solution. The solution can be found with a tool called intelligence. "I was afraid of hand-to-hand fight and fighting enemy from the vicinity. What if I can fight my enemy from distance?" Muffle mused in his mind. Suddenly his face lit up. He sprung up on his feet and started searching for some tools.

Meanwhile El was thinking about the fight he lost. His tribe had no other choice. They had nowhere to go. He had to make a choice. It must be a gamble of life. The nature presented an opportunity for them to survive and he needed to grab it. He ordered the tribe to prepare for another attack. It was all or nothing. "If we win, we can have the place we looked for our entire life. If not, we all will die. I am ready to make this gamble for survival. Last time, we were taken by surprise. But this time they don't have that advantage. I am counting on it." El mused in his mind. The sun was at its zenith. The place was bright and the Cro-Magnons went into the forest for round two. The Cro-Magnons strode across the trees stomping their feet hard on the ground. They were announcing their arrival to the Neanderthals and the Neanderthals heard it. The Neanderthals gathered before the Cro-Magnons. There was twice the Neanderthals for each Cro-Magnon. The Neanderthals pounded on the ground and growled at the

Cro-Magnons. El roared at the Neanderthals and screamed, "Kill them all.".

The two groups collided and started bashing each other dow

n. El moved forward incapacitating the Neanderthals. A neanderthal charged towards El from a tree. El swung his saw in elevation and hacked the Neanderthal mid air and started fighting another one. Like him other Cro-Magnons fought with all they got. A seeker of Cro-Magnon was fighting a Neanderthal. The Cro-Magnon swirled the spear fast such that the Neanderthal had no opening to attack. When the Neanderthal was focused on attacking and let his guard down, the seeker plunged his spear into the flank of the Neanderthal. He pulled it out while twisting it, killing the Neanderthal instantly. Slowly the Cro-Magnons started gaining the upper hand. At once, a neanderthal appeared out of nowhere. Unlike the other Neanderthals he was so big, taller than El. He charged at El with a great momentum. When El swung his saw for defence, the giant Neanderthal caught it with a hand and broke the weapon with the other hand. El started hitting the Neanderthal with his bare hand, but the Neanderthal felt nothing. The giant yanked the legs of El. El fell down hard on the ground. The giant stomped over the chest of El with his colossal feet and growled. El grunted in pain and tried to push his feet, but everything was in vain. The giant lifted a boulder nearby from ground and was about to crush El's skull with the boulder. Muffle arrived at the place. He carried a long wood curved at both ends. The ends were connected with elastic vine. It was a bow. He also carried some arrow which he made out of wood.

Muffle saw the giant trying to kill El. It was his chance to prove his worth. He crouched low with his torso perpendicular to ground. He looked sharp as his target was far away from him. The situation was same like that night when he faced the sabre tooth. He had that feeling again. He was afraid. But this time one thing is different, he had a solution. He could fight from distance. His hands did not tremble. He placed the kilt of the wooden arrow in the vine with his right hand. The giant raised the boulder above his head to crush El. Muffle pulled the vine further back and launched the arrow. The arrow whooshed through air towards the giant and harpooned through the giant's heart. The giant dropped the boulder on the ground. Blood splurged out of the giants wound and he dropped dead on ground. Seeing the incident, the Neanderthals halted their attack and fled that place. El got up and looked at the fleeing Neanderthals. One Cro-Magnon asked El whether they would come back. "Seeing now they fear us, they would come back for sure. For now, we got what we wanted to survive." El retorted. El looking at Muffle from distance nodded his head thanking him. Muffle nodded back.

This is an example how humans used fear to survive for such a long period. If you want to succeed, fear the outcome. The fear will drive to use all in your arsenal to ensure your win. This theory is even similar like Yerkes and Dodson law. Fear is the primal instinct of all lives, which can be used as a great weapon both for good and bad. In modern world, we shall use it for good.